Margaret Elizabeth Munson Sangster

On the Road Home

Poems

Margaret Elizabeth Munson Sangster

On the Road Home
Poems

ISBN/EAN: 9783337419684

Printed in Europe, USA, Canada, Australia, Japan

Cover: Foto ©Andreas Hilbeck / pixelio.de

More available books at **www.hansebooks.com**

ON THE ROAD HOME

Poems

BY

MARGARET E. SANGSTER

" East or West hame is best "

ILLUSTRATED

NEW YORK

HARPER AND BROTHERS

MDCCCXCIII

TO

MY FRIEND

HARRIET PRESCOTT SPOFFORD

The poems in this volume originally appeared in HARPER'S BAZAR and WEEKLY, *The Congregationalist, The Christian Intelligencer, Ladies' Home Journal, Home - Maker,* and *Sunday-School Times.*

CONTENTS

I—FOR SIX DAYS OUT OF SEVEN

II — LOOKING UPWARD

III — THANKSGIVING

IV — CHRISTMAS SONGS

V — EASTER

THE SIN OF OMISSION

It isn't the thing you do, Dear,
  It's the thing you leave undone
That gives you a bit of a heartache
  At the setting of the sun.
The tender word forgotten ;
  The letter you did not write ;
The flower you did not send, Dear,
  Are your haunting ghosts at night.

The stone you might have lifted
  Out of a brother's way ;
The bit of heartsome counsel
  You were hurried too much to say ;
The loving touch of the hand, Dear,
  The gentle, winning tone
Which you had no time nor thought for
  With troubles enough of your own.

Those little acts of kindness
  So easily out of mind,
Those chances to be angels
  Which we poor mortals find,

A   I

They come in night and silence,
  Each sad, reproachful wraith,
When hope is faint and flagging
  And a chill has fallen on faith.

For life is all too short, Dear,
  And sorrow is all too great
To suffer our slow compassion
  That tarries until too late ;
And it isn't the thing you do, Dear,
  It's the thing you leave undone
Which gives you a bit of a heartache
  At the setting of the sun.

HIS FIRST LOVE

His first love? Yes, I knew her very well—
 Yes, she was young and beautiful, like you;
With cheeks rose-flushed, and lovely eyes that
  fell
If people praised her overmuch, but true
And fearless, flashing out as blue eyes can
At any cruelty to beast or man.

Her voice? 'Twas very gentle, sweet and low,
 With tones to hush a tired child to sleep;
In every cadence clear, its silvery flow
 Beside a sick-bed had a charm so deep
Its spell could banish creeping waves of pain,
Bring easeful quiet to the fevered brain.

Her hands? Well, dear, they were not quite
  so small
 As those that trifle with your dainty laces;
A little browned, perhaps, they had such call
 To carry sunshine into shady places;
Less delicate than yours, and yet I doubt
If one who loved her ever found it out.

3

Her feet? Sure never steps so swift and steady
   Went straight as arrow flying to a goal;
If duty summoned her, the ever ready
   To minister to any ailing soul.
Dear feet that followed where the Master led,
And set their prints where first He'd left His
      tread!

His first love? Oh, you do begin to see
   That he might love her dearly, and that yet
His manhood's love to you might guerdon be,
   Upon your woman's brow, its coronet.
Dear girl, accept the gift. There is no other
First love so holy as *she* gained—his mother.

INTANGIBLE

PATIENTLY over the road we fare,
  Intent on the end we'd win;
There's a hint of frost in the misty air,
  And the night is closing in;
But vague and far from the muffled past
  Comes a tender, haunting tone,
And we grasp the skirts of a memory fast,
  From the land of our morning blown.

'Tis the faint, sweet sound of a tinkling bell
  Over the pastures borne;
'Tis the lamb's low bleat on the lonesome fell;
  'Tis a rustle amid the corn;
The scud and rush of the squirrel's tread
  Parting the withered leaves,
Or the twitter of swallows overhead
  In the dusk of the cottage eaves.

And once again we are boys and girls
  In a round of school and play,

5

With a mother's hand on our tangled curls,
  When we kneel at her lap to pray.
Nothing we reck of the ring of gold,
  Nor the fall of the dice on 'Change,
For the beautiful story is all untold,
  And the world yet new and strange.

And lo! instead of the masks we wear
  In the throngs we meet to-day,
Instead of the shoulders bowed to bear,
  And the eyes no longer gay,
Our cheeks are quick with the sudden flush,
  We are eager for work and strife,
And never a sorrow has come to hush
  Our jubilant pulse of life.

We sometimes catch in the crowded street
  A dear pet name we knew,
Ere the dance had gone from the childish feet,
  Or we'd gathered a sprig of rue;
'Tis somebody else who claims it now,
  But the spell of the old-time tone
Brings unawares unto lip and brow
  The light of another zone.

Faring apace to the end—'tis true,
  Yet ever behind us lies
The shimmering pearl and the fathomless blue
  Of the lucent morning skies.

And the wealth we prize as first and best
  Is a wealth no scales can weigh,
For 'tis not in the East, and not in the West,
  And not on the earth to-day.

THE PASSING YEAR

By the glimmer of green and golden,
　The leap and the sparkle of spray,
By the heart of the rose unfolden
　To the breath of the summer day.
By the shout and song of the reapers
　Binding the ripened sheaf,
By the bloom on the fragrant cluster,
　By the fall of the loosened leaf,
By the feathery whirl of the winter,
　And the deep waves' hollow sound,
By the moan of the wind in the forest
　When the night was gathering round.
By the sweet of the honey of lilies,
　By the fields all brown and sere,
Through the march of the changing seasons,
　We measured the passing year.

By the baby's step on the carpet,
　By her earliest broken word ;
And her laugh as she ran to meet us—
　Merrier never was heard,

By the time when she said, "Our Father,"
 With two little hands held up,
And the flower-face softly bending
 Like a blossom's brimming cup,
By the day she was parched with fever,
 And spent with the stress of pain,
By the hour we gave thanksgiving
 That baby was well again,
By the hide and seek of her dimples,
 And the start of her April tear,
By the grace of our darling's growing
 We measured the passing year.

By the love that is tried and precious,
 And needful as daily bread,
By the fond hands clasped in ours,
 As the chequered path we tread,
By the glow of the household faces,
 And the hush of the household peace,
By the beautiful wifely presence,
 That gives to care surcease,
By the looks that are ever tender,
 The kiss that is always true,
By the small familiar sayings,
 And the work we daily do,
By board and loaf and flagon,
 And the coming of kindred dear,
The home's unwritten story,
 We've measured the passing year.

9

By the brave things thought or spoken,
  By the true deeds simply done,
By the mean things crushed and conquered
  And the bloodless battles won,
By the days when the load was heavy,
  Yet the heart grew strong to bear,
By the days when the heart was craven,
  Lacking the strength of prayer.
By the hour that crept slow-footed,
  And the hour that flew on wings,
The time when the harp was silent,
  The time when we swept the strings.
By the dearth, the dole, and the labor,
  The fulness, reward, and cheer,
By the book of the angel's record
  We measured the passing year.

By the joy of the Christmas carols,
  And the solemn shade of the cross,
By the breaking dawn of Easter,
  And the gain that follows loss.
By the name of the world's Redeemer,
  And the sins we trample down,
By the light that shines above us,
  Though the darkling cloud may frown,
By the silent voices calling,
  By the dear remembered eyes,
By the heaven which ever beckons,
  Beyond these earthly skies,

By credos grand and steadfast,
  Banishing doubt and fear,
By the Christian's hope and comfort,
  We've measured the passing year.

THE DEAR LITTLE WIFE AT HOME

THE dear little wife at home, John,
 With ever so much to do,
Stitches to set, and babies to pet,
 And so many thoughts of you—
The beautiful household fairy,
 Filling your heart with light;
Whatever you meet to-day, John,
 Go cheerily home to-night.

For though you are worn and weary,
 You needn't be cross or curt;
There are words like darts to gentle hearts,
 There are looks that wound and hurt.
With the key in the latch at home, John,
 Drop troubles out of sight;
To the dear little wife who is waiting,
 Go cheerily home to-night.

You know she will come to meet you,
 A smile on her sunny face;
And your wee little girl, as pure as a pearl,
 Will be there in her childish grace;

12

And the boy, his father's pride, John,
  With eyes so brave and bright;
From the strife and the din to the peace, John,
  Go cheerily home to-night.

What though the tempter try you,
  Though the shafts of adverse fate
May bustle near, and the sky be drear,
  And the laggard fortune wait?
You are passing rich already,
  Let the haunting fears take flight;
With the fate that wins success, John,
  Go cheerily home to-night.

IF MOTHER WOULD LISTEN

IF mother would listen to me, dears,
   She would freshen that faded gown ;
She would sometimes take an hour's rest,
   And sometimes a trip to town.
And it shouldn't be all for the children,
   The fun and the cheer and the play ;
With the patient droop on the tired mouth,
   And the " mother has had her day."

True, mother has had her day, dears,
   When you were her babies three,
And she stepped about the farm and the house,
   As busy as ever a bee.
When she rocked you all to sleep, dears,
   And sent you all to school,
And wore herself out, and did without,
   And lived by the Golden Rule.

And so your turn has come, dears,
   Her hair is growing white,
And her eyes are gaining that far-away look
   That peers beyond the night.

14

One of these days in the morning,
    Mother will not be here;
She will fade away into silence,
    The mother so true and dear.

Then what will you do in the daylight,
    And what in the gloaming dim?
And father tired and lonesome then,
    Pray what will you do for him?
If you want to keep your mother,
    You must make her rest to-day;
Must give her a share in the frolic,
    And draw her into the play.

And if mother would listen to me, dears,
    She'd buy her a gown of silk,
With buttons of royal velvet,
    And ruffles as white as milk.
And she'd let you do the trotting,
    While she sat still in the chair;
That mother should have it hard all through,
    It strikes me isn't fair.

PATIENT WITH THE LIVING

Sweet friend, when thou and I are gone
  Beyond earth's weary labor,
When small shall be our need of grace
  From comrade or from neighbor,
Past all the strife, the toil, the care,
  And done with all the sighing,
What tender ruth shall we have gained,
  Alas, by simply dying!

Then lips too chary for their praise
  Will tell our merits over,
And eyes too swift our faults to see
  Shall no defect discover.
Then hands that would not lift a stone
  Where stones were thick to cumber
Our steep hill path, will scatter flowers
  Above our pillowed slumber.

Sweet friend, perchance both thou and I,
  Ere love is past forgiving,
Should take the earnest lesson home—
  Be patient with the living.

16

To-day's repressed rebuke may save
  Our blinding tears to-morrow;
Then patience, e'en when keenest edge
  May whet a nameless sorrow.

'Tis easy to be gentle when
  Death's silence shames our clamor,
And easy to discern the best
  Through memory's mystic glamour;
But wise it were for thee and me,
  Ere love is past forgiving,
To take the · tender lesson home—
  Be patient with the living.

B

IN THE NIGHT SEASON

You are face to face with trouble,
  And the skies are murk and gray;
You hardly know which way to turn,
  You are almost dazed, you say.
And at night you wake to wonder
  What the next day's news will bring;
Your pillow is brushed by phantom care
  With a grim and ghastly wing.

You are face to face with trouble;
  A child has gone astray;
A ship is wrecked on the bitter sea;
  There's a note you cannot pay.
Your brave right hand is feeble;
  Your sight is growing blind;
Perhaps a friend is cold and stern,
  Who was ever warm and kind.

You are face to face with trouble!
  No wonder you cannot sleep;
But stay; and think of the promise,
  The Lord will safely keep

And lead you out of the thicket,
  And into the pasture land;
You have only to walk straight onward,
  Holding the dear Lord's hand.

Face to face with trouble;
  And did you forget to look,
As the good old father taught you,
  For help to the dear old Book?
You have heard the tempter whisper;
  And you've had no heart to pray;
And God was dropped from your scheme of
      life,
  Oh! for many a weary day!

Then face to face with trouble;
  It is thus He calls you back
From the land of dearth and famine
  To the land that has no lack.
You would not hear in the sunshine,
  You hear in the midnight gloom;
Behold, His tapers kindle
  Like stars in the quiet room.

Oh! face to face with trouble,
  Friend, I have often stood;
To learn that pain hath sweetness,
  To know that God is good.

Arise and meet the daylight;
  Be strong, and do your best!
With an honest heart, and a childlike faith
  That God will do the rest.

THE GAIN OF LOSS

We hollowed the bed for our darling's rest,
  And lined it with roses white and red,
And the sod above it we softly pressed.
  "Sleep well," through our gathering tears,
        we said.
But, oh! the desolate hours we spent
In the silent home from which baby went.

We missed the patter of little feet,
  And the broken music of baby talk ;
We were lost for the cares that had been so
        sweet,
  When the fearless laddie began to walk,
And scarce could feel that another Hand
Was guiding him now in the better land.

The lonely days, and the lonely nights ;
  Had they ever a gain our fond hearts knew?
Ah, yes! for oft, from the heavenly heights,
  Came echoes floating our darkness through ;
And the land beyond grew near and bright,
Where our beautiful baby lived in light.

And our lives were touched by a holier grace,
  And each to each was bound the more,
For the dream in our souls of a little face,
  Waiting for us on the farther shore;
And day by day we heard the chime
Of bells beyond this passing time.

There came to us, too, from the baby's grave,
  A tender thought for those who wept,
And our hands were swifter to bless and save,
  Our hearts in yearning love were kept;
We were fain to cure each bitter ache,
Or ease its smart, for baby's sake.

And so we have learned to count the gain,
  Where once we counted alone the loss;
And so, through the bittersweet of pain,
  Have found the blessing within the cross.
"Thank God," we cry, with reverent breath,
"For the life that is quickened but through
      death!"

THE WIND ACROSS THE WHEAT

You ask me for the sweetest sound mine
    ears have ever heard?
A sweeter than the ripples' plash, or trilling
    of a bird,
Than tapping of the rain-drops upon the roof
    at night,
Than the sighing of the pine-trees on yon-
    der mountain height?
And I tell you, these are tender, yet never
    quite so sweet
As the murmur and the cadence of the wind
    across the wheat.

Have you watched the golden billows in a
    sunlit sea of grain,
Ere yet the reaper bound the sheaves, to fill
    the creaking wain?
Have you thought how snow and tempest,
    and the bitter wintry cold,
Were but the guardian angels, the next year's
    bread to hold?

A precious thing, unharmèd by the turmoil
  of the sky,
Just waiting, growing, silently, until the storms
  went by !

Oh ! have you lifted up your heart, to Him
  who loves us all,
And listens, through the angel-songs, if but
  a sparrow fall ?
And then, thus thinking of His hand, what
  symphony so sweet
As the music in the long refrain, the wind
  across the wheat ?

It hath its dulcet echoes, from many a lullaby,
Where the cradled babe is hushed beneath
  the mother's loving eye.
It hath its heaven-promise, as sure as heaven's
  throne,
That He who sent the manna, will ever feed
  His own ;
And, though an atom only, 'mid countless
  hosts who share
The Maker's never-ceasing watch, the Father's
  deathless care,
That atom is as dear to Him, as my dear
  child to me ;
He cannot lose me from my place, through
  all eternity :

You wonder, when it sings me *this*, there's
    nothing half so sweet,
Beneath the circling planets, as the wind
    across the wheat ?

THE HELP THAT COMES TOO LATE

'Tis a wearisome world, this world of ours,
  With its tangles small and great,
Its weeds that smother the springing flow-
        ers,
  And its hapless strifes with fate;
But the darkest day of its desolate days
  Sees the help that comes too late.

Ah! woe for the word that is never said
  Till the ear is deaf to hear,
And woe for the lack to the fainting head
  Of the ringing shout of cheer;
Ah! woe for the laggard feet that tread
  In the mournful wake of the bier.

What booteth help when the heart is numb?
  What booteth a broken spar
Of love thrown out when the lips are dumb,
  And life's barque drifted far,
Oh! far and fast from the alien past,
  Over the moaning bar?

A pitiful thing the gift to-day
   That is dross and nothing worth,
Though if it had come but yesterday,
   It had brimmed with sweet the earth ;
A fading rose in a death-cold hand,
   That perished in want and dearth.

· Who fain would help in this world of ours,
   Where sorrowful steps must fall,
Bring help in time to the waning powers
   Ere the bier is spread with the pall ;
Nor send reserves when the flags are furled,
   And the dead beyond your call.

For baffling most in this dreary world,
   With its tangles small and great,
Its lonesome nights and its weary days,
   And its struggles forlorn with fate,
Is that bitterest grief, too deep for tears,
   Of the help that comes too late.

WAITING FOR THE ANGELS

WAITING through days of fever,
Waiting through nights of pain,
   For the waft of wings at the portal,
   For the sound of songs immortal,
And the breaking of life's long chain.

There is little to do for our dear one—
Only to watch and pray—
   As the tide is outward drifting,
   As the gates of heaven are lifting,
And its gleam is on her way.

The tasks that so often taxed her,
The children she held so dear,
   The strain of the coming and going,
   The stress of the mending and sewing,
The burden of many a year.

Trouble her now no longer,
She is past the fret and care.
   On her brow is the angel's token,
   The look of a peace unbroken.
She was never before so fair.

You see she is waiting the angels,
And we—we are standing apart.
  For us there are loss and sorrow;
  For her is the endless morrow,
And the reaping-time of the heart.

WHITTIER

SEPTEMBER 7, 1892

His fourscore years and five
  Are gone, like a tale that is told.
The quick tears start, there's an ache at the
     heart,
  For we never thought him old.

Straight as a mountain pine,
  With the mountain eagle's eye,
With the hand-clasp strong, and the unhushed
     song,
  Was it time for him to die?

Prophet and priest he stood
  In the storm of embattled years;
The broken chain was his harp's refrain,
  And the peace that is balm for tears.

The hills and the valleys knew
  The poet who kept their tryst.
To our common life and our daily strife,
  He brought the blessing of Christ.

And we never thought him old,
  Though his locks were white as snow.
O heart of gold, grown suddenly cold,
  It was not time to go!

TENNYSON

" Sunset and evening star,
And one clear call for me ;
And may there be no moaning of the bar
When I put out to sea."

THERE was no moaning of the bar,
  O singer lost from sight,
When out beyond our evening star,
  Death drifted thee to light.

Black was the pilot at the helm ;
  Dark gloomed the hither shore ;
But never wave could overwhelm,
  The land that gleamed before.

Beyond these voices there is peace !
  Life fills thy cup this day !
From pain and weariness surcease
  They find who pass this way !

Oh ! laurelled at the head and feet,
  We cannot call thee dead !
Our hearts repeat thy music sweet,
  And we are comforted.

32

A BALLAD OF MAY

WE were ploughing the far - hill meadow,
    Abner, Reuben, and I,
  In the flush of the sweet May morning,
    and the off-horse balked at the rise
Midway in the longest furrow ; and I patted
    and coaxed him on ;
  I remember the scent of the brown earth,
    the blue of the bending skies.

Said Abner : " We'll rest for the nooning ;
    Old Don's in an ugly mood.
  No wonder he's tired, poor fellow ; the colt
    doesn't do his share.
I know how a horse feels, David, with a
    stubborn drop in his blood,
  When his mate is a bit of a shirk, Dave.
    I tell you it isn't fair !"

I was ready to flare in a moment ; you see,
    I was fond of the colt.
  I had trained him myself. He was flighty
    and full of kittenish pranks.

And he didn't know, and *I* didn't know, my
    dear little black Ben Bolt,
  How grave and steady he'd grow yet,
    trained in the cavalry ranks.

For swift through the sweet May morning
    came the flying thunder of hoofs,
  And "Dave! Dave! Dave!" called my
    neighbor, Jonathan Bell.
It was hurry and scurry and hasten, "Arm
    for your fields and your roofs!"
  And I left the boys and the ploughing,
    and galloped away pell-mell.

Do you know the blue Shenandoah, with its
    loops and twists of light,
  Its foams of torrent, its gleams, its brawls,
    its sheen through the fields of wheat?
All through our mountain valley we were
    up, as we thought, for the right,
  Our hearts and our wills were tempered to
    the glow of a fierce white-heat.

The bluecoats were swarming near us. Over
    our winding ways
  Glittered their dark battalions, and the flag
    we used to love

34

Flaunted its stern defiance through the grim
 and passionate days
 When men did the desperate fighting, and
 women sought God above.

Well, it's all past! Heaven be thanked, boys.
 But there's never a Southern May,
 Sweet with the lilac and jasmine, that I do
 not live again
 Through the anger and storm and madness,
 and the rollicking times and gay,
 When I was a boy on my black Ben Bolt,
 off in that hot campaign.

I am glad the flag of my fathers still waves
 o'er my native land.
 And that grave? That my little maid
 Ethel covers with flowers to-day.
 Don't laugh! You fellows are heartless.
 Yet how should *you* understand?
 That's Ben Bolt's grave in the meadow.
 We buried him there one May.

I'm grizzled and tough as a pine knot, and
 I limp a little, of course.
 But I'd never have won my wife there,
 and the children on my knee

35

Would have called some other man father,
    but for the brave black horse,
Who carried me safe through shot and
    shell, whatever our fate might be.

Battle and march and ambush, I and my
    black Ben Bolt,
We scrambled it through together, and we
    both went back to the plough,
But Abner and Rube were dead, boys! I
    tell you that Morgan colt
Had stuff in him hard to beat, and I wish
    he were living now!

THEN AND NOW

G. A. R.—WASHINGTON, 1892

FROM the wide and wind-swept prairies,
   From the rugged sea-blown coast,
From the uplands and the lowlands,
   They thronged in a mighty host.
Forth from the towns and cities,
   With the speed of the rushing train,
They hurried, the dear old fellows,
   To answer the roll again.

They fell into line and column,
   Regiment and brigade,
With the gallant colors streaming,
   And the fiery music played.
And they marched as in the old time,
   Though here was the tap of a crutch,
And there was the droop of an empty sleeve
   Tangling the heart in its clutch.

The heaven of mid-September
   Beamed over them, blue and bland,
And women smiled their welcomes,
   And children waved a hand.

There were mirth and greetings only
    In the wake of this latest camp,
Though the death-thinned ranks remembered
    The past in that sturdy tramp—

Remembered a long procession,
    Staggering, sore bespent,
Back from a hundred battles,
    With banners grimed and rent.
Boys with their gaunt pale faces,
    The friends of hunger and thirst ;
Men who had looked through the gates of
        hell
    And dared the devil his worst.

Up from the Mississippi,
    From the flame-scarred Georgian track,
From the Wilderness, and from Gettys-
        burg,
    Those soldiers came toiling back.
Are these the same, one marvels ;
    Does the old light gleam and shine,
As they follow the fife and bugle
    In the long, unwavering line ?

Aye, verily ! Here are the comrades
    With brown heads turned to gray,
And lint-white locks have the gray-beards,
    Strong in that elder day.

They left their youth behind them
    In the tempest of years agone,
When sweet out of War's rough cradle
    Slipped Peace in the breaking dawn.

Hats off!   There's a greater army
    Unstirred in its silent sleep
By the ponderous tread of the living
    And the cannons' thunder deep.
An army that keeps its muster
    On stones that as sentries stand,
With the names of tens of thousands,
    The flower of all the land.

The winds are forever chanting
    A requiem for these ;
Brave autumn flaunts their banners
    In the flushing maple-trees ;
And the glad birds, winging southward,
    Over them pause and rest,
Dropping a song for love, above
    The flower of East and West.

A truce to memory's dreaming !
    O flag that we live to serve ;
By all we hold most holy,
    Never from thee we'll swerve !

Dear flag that rallies a nation,
  A mighty, growing host
From the breezy, rippling prairies
  To the rugged sea-blown coast.

THE EVENING LESSON

In hands that are gnarled with labor,
   And swart with the kiss of the sun,
She is holding her worn old Bible
   When the day is almost done.
And, gazing through misty glasses,
   For her eyes are growing dim,
She thinks of the Lord who has led her,
   And the way she has walked with Him.

The hills in the purple distance
   Looked over her childish head:
No charm from their brows has faded,
   No tint of their glory fled.
And the sweet green-waving meadows
   Through the long years reaped and sown,
For all their harvest guerdons
   No blight of age have known.

But she can scarce remember,
   It went so long ago,
The time of the tripping footstep,
   And the heart's exultant glow.

The life has been hard and bitter,
  With its tasks and dull routine,
Less of a song than a sermon,
  And the rests so few between.

And yet, she has walked with the Mas-
    ter ;
  He has come at the even-tide
To comfort her with His presence.
  He has lingered oft by her side
In the hour of care and sorrow,
  And the burden has not pressed
So heavily at His whisper,
  " Lo ! I will give you rest !"

She read just now in the chapter
  Where her ribbon marker lies,
Of the flow of the crystal river,
  And the never-darkened skies.
In her there is less of longing
  For the golden-paven street,
Than for somewhere a little refuge
  Low at the Saviour's feet.

She has even a quiver of shyness
  For the angels at the gate,
And the splendid stately choirs
  At the great white throne who wait,

And yearns for a tiny corner
  To hide herself away,
Till she feels at home in heaven,
  In the wonderful, peaceful day.

Dear soul, trust Him who loveth
  His own to the very end,
Who, alike for earth and heaven,
  Is thine unfailing Friend.
He will lift the latest burden,
  And loose thy sandal-shoon,
And give thee youth and freedom
  In His own good time, and soon.

Reading the evening lesson
  In a simple, childlike way,
She gathers strength for the labor
  Of each revolving day.
She never has time in the morning,
  When the work must all be done,
But she keeps her tryst with the Master
  At the setting of the sun.

BELLS IN THE DESERT

Above, the desert's mocking sky ;
  Below, the desert's sand ;
No palm's green fringe to rest the eye,
  No fruit to fill the hand.

But on the pilgrim's raptured ear,
  In liquid, silvery swells
Oh, faint and far, yet sweet and clear,
  The sound of Sabbath bells.

Across the brooding desert-gloom
  The matchless music floats,
The fragrance of the clover's bloom
  Is in the lingering notes.

Athwart the dark sirocco's drift
  The thought of home is borne ;
Once more their wings the robins lift
  Above the springing corn.

No count of dreary days he keeps,
　The weary leagues along,
When lo! o'er flesh and spirit sweeps
　A tide of hallowed song.

The sweet bells chime ; his sister blends
　Her voice amid their waves,
O'er half the world Balerma sends
　The call of Him who saves.

A space, the airy music dies,
　And silence reigns supreme.
Once more, the sand, the empty skies,
　The fading of a dream.

Yet, bravely heartened, on he goes,
　As girded on with strength,
Nor fears the rush of sudden foes,
　Nor dreads the journey's length.

The thought of home, the vision pure,
　Have cheered the toilsome way,
And nerved the pilgrim to endure
　The trials of the day.

Ah! comrades, in this world of pain
　What courage, hope, and cheer,
The bells of heaven with sweet refrain
　Sound on the listening ear.

We hear them when our lips are dumb,
  When life is dull and gray,
God's loving messengers, they come,
  God's wondrous words they say.

Perchance the hands of dear ones gone
  Touch soft the vibrant strings,
Or, angels of the immortal dawn,
  Draw near on soundless wings.

To us alone the song is sent,
  The wine for us is poured,
We rise, and forward fare, content—
  Our eyes have seen the Lord.

A LESSON

My little laddie with the earnest eyes
  Had toiled an hour to build a castle fair;
I watched each bridge and tower and turret
    rise,
  Then saw him slowly make a winding stair.

Most beautiful the castle was to see!
  A wee flag floating from the battlement!
Alas! my hasty touch! Ah! woe is me,
  The whole frail fabric into ruins went!

One instant anger lit the childish face,
  Quick tears sprang up to quench the dark
    eyes light;
And then, with wonderful, imperial grace,
  He curbed that fiery spirit in my sight.

"*You didn't mean to!* Never mind," he said.
  "I'll build a prettier castle by and by;"
Then, with a swift shake of the sunny head,
  "Why, Dearie, *never* mind! You *shouldn't*
    cry!"

Brave little hero, may I be as strong,
  As swift and ready in self-mastery,
Whene'er in this world's course mistake or
      wrong
  Upsets some castle just as dear to me!

CHRYSANTHEMUMS

WITH summer and sun behind you,
  With winter and shade before,
You crowd in your regal splendor
  Through the autumn's closing door.
White as the snow that is coming,
  Red as the rose that is gone,
Gold as the heart of the lilies,
  Pink as the flush of the dawn.
Confident, winsome, stately,
  You throng in the wane of the year.
Trooping an army with banners
  When the leafless woods are sere.

Sweet is your breath as of spices
  From a far sea island blown ;
Chaste your robes as of vestals
  Trimming their lamps alone.
Strong are your hearts, and sturdy
  The life that in root and stem
Smoulders and glows till it sparkles
  In each flowery diadem.

Nothing of bloom and odor
   Have your peerless legions lost,
Marching in fervid beauty
   To challenge the death-white frost.

So to the eye of sorrow
   Ye bring a flicker of light;
The cheek that was wan with illness
   Smiles at your faces bright.
The children laugh in greeting,
   And the dear old people say,
"Here are the self-same darlings
   We loved in our own young day,"
As, summer and sun behind you,
   Winter and shade before,
You crowd in your regal splendor
   Through the autumn's closing door.

IN THE BELFRY

CLIMB up the dusky turret stair
  Ere yet the dawn of day,
And set the silent bells to speech,
  That near and far away
All waking things may hear the joy
  Pulsating in the air,
As Freedom's silver chimes exult
  For Freedom everywhere.

Climb up the narrow turret stair, .
  Oh, ringer, haste to climb!
The bells shall ring for answered prayer
  Adown the aisles of Time.
In this dear Western land of ours,
  Still let the tale be told,
That Freedom's self we dearer prize
  Than misers prize their gold.

Climb up the haunted belfry stair!
  A hundred years ago
A boy's blithe ringing struck the peal
  That challenged friend and foe ;

The flag flung out its vivid folds,
  And forth from many a spire
The answering bells in music broke
  To greet the land's desire.

Climb up the echoing turret stair,
  And ring the bells once more.
From sea to sea, from lip to lip,
  Oh, bid the joy run o'er!
Dear land that Godward looks to-day,
  Dear land that childward bends,
Thine be the call our hearts obey
  Full gladly till life ends.

IN HAMPTON ROADS

APRIL, 1893

BLUE sky above, blue sea below,
  A rainbow flutter from fort and fleet,
Flashing of signals to and fro,
  And the ocean highway a thronging street.

Banners flung on the April air,
  Thunder of cannon in blithe salute,
The drum's deep note and the trumpet's blare,
  The mellow music of pipe and flute.

Seafaring men, with faces tanned
  By sun and tempest and windy weather,
A chain of commerce that land with land
  Links the states of the world together.

And back of it all, to-day, one sees
The swart, stern brow of the Genoese ;
And under it all, to day, one hears
The diapason of time's long years.

FLOWERS FOR MEMORIAL DAY

COME hither, little darling, and help me gather
    bloom—
Great roses, soaked with sunshine, and the
    lilac's purple plume ;
For the banners will be waving, the stormy
    drums will beat,
And the tread of marching regiments will
    shake the listening street ;
And you will clap your hands, dear, the
    world will be so gay,
The shops and schools all closed in town,
    this bright Memorial Day.

You ask what 'tis about, dear, and why we
    pick the flowers,
And break the long, green branches, dew-
    gemmed in fragrant showers ;
Why we always take the same path, and
    seek the solemn place
Where rows and rows of narrow graves are
    marshalled in one space,

As if a regiment of dead were sleeping there
    together,
As many a time in life they slept, unheed-
    ing wind or weather.

Hear this, my bonny darling; you're old
    enough to know
That once these sleeping soldiers grimly faced
    a living foe.
My father was among them, and I, a child
    like you,
Gave him a good-bye kiss, dear, when he
    wore our country's blue.
He caught me in his arms, dear, and his
    bearded cheek was wet;
That parting kiss and clasp, my child, I
    never could forget.
He loved these dear spring flowers, the lilacs
    best of all,
And we'll cover up his bed with them—a
    royal purple pall.

Halt! Why, the men are coming; they are
    just beyond the door.
Run out, my little one, and strew the flowers
    their feet before,
And wave your dimpled hand, dear, to the
    banner of the stars.
There is no flag so splendid, worth the heart-
    aches and the scars,

Worth all it cost to save it, worth all our
    love and pride—
The banner brave men live for, and for
    which brave men died.

And oft as spring returns, dear, and decks
    the smiling land,
Till the blossoms break and ripple, like the
    foam upon the strand,
Whatever else we do, dear, whatever leave
    undone,
We'll keep in sacred memory the men whose
    fields are won.
We'll ask our God to make us as pure
    and brave as they
On whose green graves we scatter bloom this
    fair Memorial Day.

CROSSING THE DOWN-TOWN FERRIES

Crossing the down-town ferries,
　　I challenge a braver sight
Than the throngs of working-people
　　Homeward faring at night.
Never a drum before them,
　　Never a banner above,
But they march to soundless music
　　Under the flag of love.

There are men with grimy faces
　　And coats that are out of date,
Women whose pallid lips and cheeks
　　Tell the dreary struggle with fate.
But oh! the cheery courage
　　And the eyes with light aglow
As over the down-town ferries
　　These toilers come and go!

They are working for wife and babies,
　　For a mother bent and gray,
Or a sister bound to a weary couch,
　　With only the strength to pray.

Working for honest wages
  To pay for the bread they eat,
Or to buy the children's school-books,
  And shoes for the children's feet.

Crossing the down-town ferries
  Daily at set of sun,
You may meet the crowds of toilers
  Whose long day's work is done.
You know what a shout of greeting
  They'll hear when they lift the latch—
A shout the angels listen for,
  And pause in their songs to catch.

Who does not thrill with pleasure
  As the brave procession comes,
Needing no rally of bugles,
  Nor beat of strenuous drums?
Though a host may press anear them
  Who neither toil nor spin,
Nor theirs to wear the laurels
  The lowlier laborers win.

II

LOOKING UPWARD

TWO OR THREE

THERE were only two or three of us,
  Who came to the place of prayer,
Came in the teeth of a driving storm,
  But for that we did not care,
Since, after our hymns of praise had risen,
  And our earnest prayers were said,
The Master Himself was present there,
  And gave us the living bread.

We knew His look in our leader's face,
  So rapt, and glad, and free ;
We felt His touch when our heads were bowed,
  We heard His "Come to Me !"
Nobody saw Him lift the latch,
  And none unbarred the door ;
But "Peace" was His token to every heart,
  And how could we ask for more ?

Each of us felt the load of sin
  From the weary shoulder fall ;
Each of us dropped the load of care,
  And the grief that was like a pall ;

And over our spirits a blessed calm
  Swept in from the jasper sea,
And strength was ours for toil and strife
  In the days that were thence to be.

It was only a handful gathered in
  To the little place of prayer;
Outside were struggle and pain and sin,
  But the Lord Himself was there;
He came to redeem the pledge He gave—
  Wherever His loved ones be,
To stand Himself in the midst of them,
  Though they count but two or three.

And forth we fared in the bitter rain,
  And our hearts had grown so warm
It seemed like the pelting of summer flowers,
  And not like the crash of a storm.
" 'Twas a time of the dearest privilege
  Of the Lord's right hand," we said,
As we thought how Jesus Himself had come
  To feed us with living bread.

TE DEUM LAUDAMUS

For our dear ones safe on the other side,
   We give Thee praise, O Lord!
Though our hearts are sore for prayers denied,
   And our songs have a broken chord.
Never the stain of shame or sin,
   Never the blight of pain,
Shall come to the blest who have entered in,
   Where only love doth reign.

Entered in to the hall of the feast,
   Through the gates of jasper clear;
Where the dear Lord's hand shall lead the
     least,
   And Himself shall to all be near.
Entered in, where the deathless life
   Into every soul is poured.
Entered, where never toil or strife
   Is seen in the light of the Lord.

Some, whom we lost in the long ago,
   Are waiting to greet us there;

Forgotten the burden of mortal woe,
  Untasted the earth's despair.
Oh! well when we kneel at the Master's feet,
  May we thank His tender love,
That saved the bitter and gave the sweet,
  In the cup they quaff above.

But thanks and praise for the dear ones gone
  To dwell in the peace of God,
No longer weary, or spent, or lone,
  No longer under the rod ;
Learning and growing day by day .
  Where they count not life by days,
Treading forever the upward way—
  For these let us offer praise.

Swiftly and surely the hour will come,
  When, dropping the load of care,
We, too, shall wing to the better home,
  And be found of the loved ones there.
For the family life, and the family love,
  Are safe in the Father's thought ;
And one and all, to His house above,
  Shall His ransomed at last be brought.

HOW LONG?

Some days when the sun is brightest,
  And the wind is soft and sweet,
When the ripples feather the lightest
  Over the ripened wheat ;
When the world is fullest of music,
  And life is thrilled with song,
The cry of my soul is lifted,
  " How long, O Lord ! how long ?"

For against the rich, blithe summer
  The pain of the world is set ;
I hear the moans of the shipwrecked,
  And the groans of vain regret,
The wail of the heavy-hearted,
  The grief of the one gone wrong,
And the cry of my soul is lifted,
  " How long, O Lord ! how long ?"

Then, stilling my thoughts that struggle,
  And bidding the tumult cease,
As sweet as an angel's whisper,
  Comes a blessed word of peace,

E   65

And the Lord Himself says, gently:
  "Hush not thy thankful song,
I am yet the Father in heaven,
  And I list to thy plaint, 'How long?' .

"In the day of the years eternal,
  Beginning and end I see,
The world is glad and sorrowful both,
  And the world is safe with Me.
The trouble and loss shall vanish;
  Believe, and await the song,
Untouched by the minor of discord,
  Where the ransomed legions throng."

GOD'S APPOINTMENTS

THIS thing on which thy heart was set, this
    thing that cannot be,
This weary, disappointing day, that dawns,
    my friend, for thee ;—
Be comforted ; God knoweth best, the God
    whose name is Love,
Whose tender care is evermore our passing
    lives above.
He sends thee disappointment ? Well, then,
    take it from His hand.
Shall God's appointment seem less good than
    what thyself had planned ?

'Twas in thy mind to go abroad. He bids
    thee stay at home ?
Oh ! happy home ; thrice happy if to it thy
    guest He come.
'Twas in thy mind thy friend to see. The
    Lord says, " Nay, not yet."
Be confident ; the meeting-time thy Lord will
    not forget.

'Twas in thy mind to work for Him. His
    will is, " Child, sit still ;"
And surely 'tis thy blessedness to mind the
    Master's will.
Accept thy disappointment, friend, thy gift
    from God's own hand.
Shall God's appointment seem less good than
    what thyself had planned ?

So, day by day and step by step, sustain thy
    failing strength,
From strength to strength, indeed, go on
    through all the journey's length.
God bids thee tarry now and then, forbear
    the weak complaint ;
God's leisure brings the weary rest, and cor-
    dial gives the faint.
God bids thee labor, and the place is thick
    with thorn and brier ;
But He will share the hardest task, until He
    calls thee higher.
So take each disappointment, friend ; 'tis at
    thy Lord's command !
Shall God's appointment seem less good than
    what thyself had planned ?

A KING'S MESSENGER

"THE King will send a messenger; set thou
    thy house in state,
And listening for His high behests, do thou
    in patience wait."
So ran the letter that she read, between the
    dawn and dark,
And her heart went forth in answer swift,
    the day of days to mark.

Soon the house was swept and garnished, and
    she filled each space with flowers,
And, singing, to and fro she passed, and chid
    the laggard hours;
Then her board was spread for feasting, and
    her flagons brimmed with wine,
For naught could be too rich or rare to
    please the guest Divine.

"The King will send a messenger, a mes-
    senger who stands
Full often where he takes the gifts of love
    from royal hands.

The King hath gift and grace for thee, have
  thou thy heart prepared ;
The precious treasure meant for *thee*, no other
  soul hath shared."

So came the second missive, between the stars
  that burn,
The steadfast warders of the night, each in
  its ordered turn ;
And she set her heart in order, she searched
  her soul to see
If any evil thing by chance in lurking haunt
  might be.

She knelt in lowly vigil, and her pleading
  prayer went forth,
But came apace no messenger from South-
  land or from North.
She questioned Life, she questioned Death, she
  asked all mystery,
But none could tell her of the gift that erst
  her own would be.

And while she waited, ill at ease, the song
  died on her lips,
The flowers faded, and the light of noonday
  knew eclipse ;

A shadow crept athwart the floor, the door
    swung open wide,
And the messenger the King had sent was
    standing at her side.

Alas! That messenger had brought a gleam-
    ing sword of woe,
That reft the golden links of love, and laid
    the dearest low.
She shivered, mute and desolate, crushed under
    blinding pain;
Could this be Heaven's messenger, to cleave
    her life in twain?

Then the day grew as the midnight, and the
    midnight as the day;
Nor sun nor stars shone over her, upon the
    weary way.
Men marked the furrowing of her brow, the
    blanching of her hair,
And the shadow deep and deeper grew, till
    night lay everywhere.

Then slowly came a marvel, a miracle to
    see,
For out of gloom a wondrous light was
    born her own to be.

There was knowledge of all suffering, that
    through the torpor stole,
Until she learned the secret of the balm that
    maketh whole.

Then the shadow changed to glory, and be-
    hold! an angel form,
With a radiance like the splendor of the
    sunlight after storm!
And ere she knew it Heaven had come within
    her home's small space,
To make, oh! strange, sweet wonder, there a
    hallowed dwelling-place.

And now the flowers are blooming, and again
    she sings by day,
And she feels the angels near her when at
    eve she kneels to pray.
She shall find the dear lost darlings, she will
    know them as they stand,
Serene and full of gladness, in the blessed
    better land.

The King *did* send a messenger, and Sorrow
    was his name,
And in his mighty hand he bore a sword of
    smiting flame.

But the sword was wreathed with lilies, and
    they will not fade away,
For they were sown in gardens where the
    flowers bloom for aye.

THE CITY OF GOD

Four square it lies, with walls of gleaming
  pearl
 And gates that are not shut at all by day:
There evermore their wings the storm winds
  furl,
 And night falls not upon the shining way
Up which by twos and threes, and in great
  throngs,
 The happy people tread, whose mortal road
Led straight to that fair home of endless
  songs,
 The city, beautiful and vast, of God.

Eye hath not seen, ear hath not heard, the
  joy,
 The light, the bloom of that sweet dwelling-place,
Where praise is aye the rapturous employ
 Of those who there behold God's loving
  face.

Here, fretted by so many a tedious care,
    And bowed by burdens on the weary road,
We cannot dream of all the glory there,
    In that bright city, beautiful, of God.

There some have waited for our coming long,
    Blown thither on the mystic tide of death,
They catch some fragments of our broken
        song,
    The while the eternal years are as a breath.
There we shall go one gladsome day of days,
    And drop forever every cumbering load,
And we shall view, undimmed by earth's
        low haze,
    The city, beautiful and vast, of God.

In that great city we shall see the King,
    And tell Him how He took us by the hand
And let us, in our weakness, drag and cling,
    As children when they do not understand,
Yet with the mother walk as night comes
        on,
    And wish that home were on some smooth-
        er road.
Oh, with what pleasure shall we look upon
    Our Saviour in the city of our God!

A SONG OF SUMMER

THE ships glide in at the harbor's mouth,
  And the ships sail out to sea,
And the wind that sweeps from the sunny
      South,
  It is sweet as sweet can be.
There's a world of toil and a world of pains,
  There's a world of trouble and care,
But oh, in a world where our Father reigns,
  There is gladness everywhere!

The harvest waves in the breezy morn,
  And the men go forth to reap;
The fulness comes to the tasselled corn,
  Whether we wake or sleep.
And far on the hills by feet untrod,
  There are blossoms that scent the air,
For oh, in this world of our Father, God,
  There is beauty everywhere!

The breath grows faint on the dying lips,
  And the weary hands lie still.
Our life is dimmed by the grief-eclipse,
  But we rest on the Father's will.

A world of parting, a world of tears,
 Yet we sink not in despair,
For oh, in the midst of the mournful years,
 There is comfort everywhere!

The babe lies soft on the mother's breast,
 And the tide of joy flows in.
He giveth, He taketh, He knoweth best,
 The Lord to whose home we win.
And oh, when the soul is with trials tossed,
 There is help in the lifted prayer!
For never a soul that He loves is lost,
 And our Father is everywhere.

The ships sail over the harbor bar
 Away and away to sea.
The ships sail in with the evening star
 To the port where no tempests be.
The harvests wave on the summer hills,
 And the bands go forth to reap,
And all is right, as our Father wills,
 Whether we wake or sleep.

A DAY OF THE LORD

IT was not a day of feasting,
  Nor a day of the brimming cup ;
There were bitter drops in the fountain
  Of life as it bubbled up,
And over the toilsome hours
  Were sorrow and weakness poured,
Yet I said " Amen," when night came ;
  It had been a day of the Lord.

A day of His sweetest whispers,
  In the hush of the tempest's whirl ;
A day when the Master's blessing
  Was pure in my hand as a pearl.
A day when, under orders,
  I was fettered, yet was free ;
A day of strife and triumph,
  A day of the Lord to me.

And my head as it touched the pillow,
  When the darkness gathered deep,
Was soothed at the thought of taking
  The gift of childlike sleep ;

For what were burdens carried,
   And what was the foeman's sword,
To one who had fought and conquered
   In a blessed day of the Lord?

THE INVISIBLE GUEST

The whole family in heaven and on earth.—*Eph. iii.* 15.

THE children gather the table round,
　And this is rosy and that is fair ;
No dearer group in the land is found,
　With their laughing eyes and their golden
　　　hair.
In its innocent freedom the household mirth
　Ripples along in a sparkling tide,
And the ruddy cheer of the firelit hearth
　Streams o'er the snow on the highway side.

But the mother turns from the curtained
　　　pane,
　And, counting her children one by one,
Sees the child who will never come back again,
　Just as if she had never gone.
And between her sisters the grave, sweet face,
　A lingering smile in the lovely eyes,
Is lighting the mother's shadowed place
　With the wonderful glory of Paradise.

So

Only a tender fancy, wrought
　　Of tissues a mother's longing weaves?
Only a picture of memory brought
　　From under the last year's withered leaves?
I like to think that the Father's love,
　　Keeping us all in its hallowed care,
Sent that sweet waft from the home above
　　To comfort the mother mourning there.

She mused but now of the little mound,
　　A gray-green scar on the furrowed turf,
The white drifts heaping its loneness round,
　　Tumbled and broken like frozen surf,
And the old pain woke; yet her gentle
　　　　thought
Was not to silence the children's glee,
When into her spirit's depth was brought
　　A word triumphant: "Lord, with Thee,

"Dear Lord, with Thee is my treasure kept,
　　Safe from the storm which sweeps the wild,
At home with Thee, for in Thee she slept,
　　And my Saviour's arms enfold my child."
How many who think of the dear ones gone,
　　Thus lift the heart to the better land—
Thus wait through the night till the new
　　　　day's dawn,
　　In the Presence where they and we shall
　　　　stand.

F   81

Their names are starred on the houshold roll;
  They mingle not in the household life;
Yet—living soul unto living soul—
  They whisper peace to our weary strife.
Not theirs to struggle for daily bread,
  To join the search for the fleeting gold;
But not a pulse of their love is dead,
  Nor ever a thought they send us cold.

Into our gay and festal days,
  As into days that are dull and gray,
They drop the sweets of the endless praise,
  Which thrills in the place where their
      angels stay.
And what though sometimes the tear-drops
      start,
  As the haunting footsteps go and come!
Their memory hallows the trusting heart,
  And bids its murmur of loss be dumb.

THEY NEITHER TOIL NOR SPIN

THEY neither toil nor spin; they wear
Their loveliness without a care;

As pure as when the Master's feet
Were set amid their perfume sweet.

The summer hills rejoice to see
Their carven censers swinging free.

They wait within the gates of dawn
Till all the watching stars are gone,

Then open cups of honey-dew,
To greet the morn's returning hue.

Oh fair, wise virgins, clothed in white;
Oh lilies, fresh from looms of light,

I dearly love you, for the word
That stars you, noted of the Lord.

I love you when, in gold and red,
The sunset colors o'er you spread;

Or when, like fairy sails of snow,
The river rocks you to and fro.

You are the Master's flowers to me;
His smile upon your grace I see.

My transient discontents I hush,
If but my garment's hem ye brush.

And everywhere your fragrance brings
This message from the King of Kings:

"We neither toil nor spin. And ye,
Who spin so long and wearily,

"Who toil amid earth's grime and dust,
Behold—a hallowed arc of trust.

"Oh, pause and hear the Father say
His angels are your guides to-day!

"While worlds in matchless order move,
Ye shall not slip from sovereign love;

"For He who bids the planets sweep,
Cares for the tiniest babe asleep."

THE CORE OF THE HOUSE

THE core of the house, the dearest place, the
    one that we all love best,
Holding it close in our heart of hearts, for
    its comfort and its rest,
Is never the place where strangers come, nor
    yet where friends are met,
Is never the stately drawing-room, where our
    treasured things are set.
Oh, dearer far, as the time recedes in a dream
    of colors dim,
Breathing across our stormy moods like the
    echo of a hymn,
Forever our own, and only ours, and pure as
    a rose in bloom,
Is the centre and soul of the old home nest,
    the mother's darling room.

We flew to its arms when we rushed from
    school, with a thousand things to tell;
Our mother was always waiting there, had
    the day gone ill or well.

No other pillow was quite so cool, under an
    aching head,
As soft to our fevered childish cheek, as the
    pillow on mother's bed.
Sitting so safely at her feet, when the dewy
    dusk drew nigh,
We watched for the angels to light the lamps
    in the solemn evening sky.
Tiny hands folded, there we knelt, to lisp the
    nightly prayer,
Learning to cast on the Loving One early
    our load of care.
Whatever the world has brought us since,
    yet, pure as a rose in bloom,
Is the thought we keep of the core of the
    home, the mother's darling room.

We think of it oft in the glare and heat of
    our lifetime's later day,
Around our steps when the wild spray beats,
    and the mirk is gathering gray.
As once to the altar's foot they ran whom
    the menacing foe pursued,
We turn to the still and sacred place where
    a foe may never intrude,
And there, in the hush of remembered hours,
    our failing souls grow strong,
And gird themselves anew for the fray, the
    battle of right and wrong,

Behind us ever the hallowed thought, as pure
  as a rose in bloom,
Of the happiest place in all the earth, the
  mother's darling room.

We've not forgotten the fragrant sheaves of
  the lilacs at the door,
Nor the ladder of sunbeams lying prone on
  the shining morning floor.
We've not forgotten the robin's tap at the
  ever friendly pane,
Nor the lilt of the little brook outside, troll-
  ing its gay refrain.
How it haunts us yet, in the tender hour of
  the sunset's fading blush,
The vesper-song, so silvery clear, of the hidden hermit-thrush !
All sweetest of sound and scent is blent,
  when, pure as a rose in bloom,
We think of the spot loved best in life, the
  mother's darling room.

Holding us close to our best in life, keeping
  us back from sin,
Folding us yet to her faithful breast, oft as
  a prize we win,
The mother who left us here alone to battle
  with care and strife
Is the guardian angel who leads us on to
  the fruit of the tree of life.

Her smile from the heights we hope to gain
    is an ever-beckoning lure ;
We catch her look when our pulses faint,
    nerving us to endure.
Others may dwell where once she dwelt, and
    the home be ours no more,
But the thought of her is a sacred spell,
    never its magic o'er.
We're truer and stronger and braver yet,
    that, pure as a rose in bloom,
Back of all struggle, a heart of peace, is the
    mother's darling room.

THE CHILD AT THE GATE

'Twas a little faint tap at the golden gate
   And St. Peter came with the key,
For never in heaven is soon or late
   Whoever may knocking be.

And all in a rift of the morning star
   A small child waited there,
On tiptoe touching the jewelled bar
   With the dew-drops caught in her hair.

A mither-bairn who had never known
   Aught save the tenderest care ;
She had fared to the heavenly land alone,
   As the souls of all must fare.

The good Saint opened wide the door,
   "Come in, there is naught to fear,
You have done with trouble forever more
   Oh ! little one, safe and here.

"Now enter in where the children play,
   And the dear Lord smiles to see

Their guileless mirth as He did in the day
  When He walked in Galilee."

A soft wind stirred in the lily beds,
  The children paused in their play,
And bent the ranks of their flaxen heads,
  As children in church who pray.

Then One drew near with the brooding eyes
  That are homes of love unpriced ;
And the little soul looked up, trustful, wise,
  Into the Face of Christ.

Across the meadows she went with Him,
  And He held her fast by the hand ;
And He gave her drink from the cups that
    brim
  With the sweet of the deathless hand.

Oh ! if the mother who waked and wept,
  By a cradle's empty space,
Had dreamed how Love had her treasure kept
  In the dear Lord's dwelling-place,

She would never have mourned so bitterly,
  Nor found it so hard to wait,
Till the good St. Peter should turn the key
  For her, in the golden gate.

OUR BROKEN DAYS

SHALL we have days unbroken,
  Nay, more, an endless day,
Where ne'er a harsh word spoken
  Shall cloud our onward way,
Where never hope shall perish,
  Nor ever grief shall moan,
Where all our fond hearts cherish
  Shall aye abide our own?

Oh! peace for which in yearning
  Our wearied spirits wait,
Oh! love whose fullest learning
  No dear desire shall sate,
Nor eye nor ear hath measured
  The glory and the praise,
Which God for us hath treasured
  Beyond these broken days.

Chill days when pulses languish,
  And mists of life hang low,
Dark days whose load of anguish
  Rolls on with sluggish flow,

And busy days whose weaving
  Stretches from sun to sun,
And days of dull believing,
  Whose tedious course is run.

The days of haste and worry
  When interruptions throng,
The days of waste and flurry
  That leave no heart for song,
The days of earthly leaven,
  And dimming worldly dross,
The empty days bereaven,
  In shadow of the cross.

Yes, these shall all be over,
  And garments bright with praise
Their memory shall cover
  Beyond our broken days.
Such petty trifles pain us,
  Here in this fevered life,
Such dragging fetters chain us,
  Our hands with care so rife,

We scarce discern how holy
  And sweet the time might be
If spent in converse lowly,
  O gracious King, with Thee.
We lose the tender gladness
  It might be ours to win,

And trail our robes in sadness,
  And stain their folds with sin.

Bless God, there's no temptation
  To snare the hearts at home,
To heaven's pure isolation
  No strife or ill shall come.
The Lord who loved and bought us
  Lays up a feast of praise,
Until He safe have brought us
  Beyond our broken days.

THE COMMUNION OF SAINTS

A THOUSAND leagues of land and sea
Divide, to-day, my friend and me.

I cannot clasp her tender hand,
Or in her gracious presence stand ;

No word of mine may reach her ear,
And yet I hold her close and dear.

In loyal thought my love is sent,
O'er mountain chain and continent ;

In vain extends the widest sea
To separate my friend and me,

Since heart to heart, o'er time and space,
Her truth is still my dwelling-place.

.   .   .   .   .   .

Where gates of chrysoprase and pearl
Their gleaming leaves of light unfurl,

94

Where evermore the glory falls
On golden floor and jewelled walls,

Where Christ Himself the ransomed praise
Through long, unclouded, sinless days—

There, safe beyond these changeful tides,
Dear as my life, a friend abides.

Not mine to touch His garment's hem,
Not mine, as yet, the floods to stem,

And on the hills forever fair
Breathe gladly love's divinest air.

But death and distance cannot part
My friend and me ; for heart to heart,

The one in heaven, the one on earth,
We share the new and royal birth.

Gone on a little while before,
My friend hath pain and pang no more.

And I, who wait till even-song
Shall waft my latest prayer along,

And carry up my praiseful breath
By some angelic wing of death,

Know well, full well, that, heart to heart,
We, parted here, but seem to part.

For since the Lord of life is King,
His pilgrims homeward pledged to bring,

Not powers beneath, nor hosts above,
Can break the triple bands of love.

There menaces, on land or sea,
No peril to my friend and me.

There is no fear, let come what will,
But I shall keep my friend, who still,

Invisible to mortal sense,
Abides, in God's good Providence,

The hour when we again shall meet.
Nay, often, at the Mercy Seat,

A hand, once pierced, unites us both ;
Beyond the reach of rust and moth

Our precious things for us are stored,
When one is present with the Lord,

And one anear the hither sea
Is—with the Lord—content to be.

MY ALABASTER BOX

It was not at meat in the Pharisee's house
  That I sought the Lord to-day,
Nor yet in my closet, hushed and fair,
  When I lowly knelt to pray,
But I carried my box of ointment sweet
In the face of the throngs that I chanced to
    meet.

"It is jewelled and precious," I proudly cried,
  "And it cost me gems and gold,
And see, I shall pour it freely out
  That my neighbors may behold,
And then I will meekly go my way.
'She has broken her box,'" will the gazers
    say.

So up and down through the busy street,
  Seeking my Lord, I went,
My head held high and my soul on fire
  With the glow of its good intent,
And presently hard where two roads met
Stood One whom my soul cannot forget.

Down in the dust at His beautiful feet,
　　With my trailing draperies white,
I cast myself with the odors sweet—
　　Were there angels to watch the sight ?—
" Lo ! I for Thy pleasing have brought my best ;
Take it, sweet Saviour, and give me rest ! "

He stayed me then with a kingly word ;
　　" Not so, my child ! " said He.
" Hast thou never a thought of the hidden
　　　　name
　　In the hands that were pierced for Thee ?
Would'st thou wound the heart that broke
　　　　to save
Thy life from the power that holds the slave ?

" Bring hither thy pride and thy discontent
　　And thy cherished and vain self-will ;
Empty thy soul of its low desires
　　That My love that soul may fill.
It is not thy jewelled box I crave ;
I am seeking the soul that I died to save.

" And never a gift of precious worth
　　Canst thou bestow upon me
While thou shuttest thy poorest brother out
　　From thy quickened sympathy,
And never in crowds and sordid show
Can I my best upon thee bestow."

The vision faded; the throng whirled by;
   I stood in the path alone.
Then I went to seek for the lost, the weak,
   Since my blessed Lord was gone.
Wherever they need me the box I break,
To-day, to-day, for my Lord's dear sake.

FAIN would I be strong with the heart of
    the brave,
  All fearless in conflict, all calm in defeat!
Fain would I be patient, Lord, patience I
    crave,
  In pain to be silent, submissive and sweet.
Oh, where shall I find it, the strength I would
    win,
  As pilgrim I journey through peril and sin?
My Master, my Saviour, my help is in Thee,
In Thee is my help, Lord, 'tis only in Thee.

Fain would I be gentle, whatever betide,
  And meek, unresisting, returning no word
In haste or in anger to those at my side
  Who may grieve or annoy me. Thy gen-
    tleness, Lord,
Bestow on thy child, that her looks may be
    fair,
And mildness distil from her speech, and
    her care

Be laid at Thy feet ; for whatever it be
In Thee is my help, Lord, and only in Thee.

Fain would I be faithful, so daily to prove
   To those whom I meet that my life has a
      spring
Abundant in beauty and precious in love,
   And that close to the Vine in my earth-
      life I cling.
Fain would I be faithful, nor follow afar,
Fain would I abide where Thy chosen ones
      are ;
My Master, my Saviour, be gracious to me,
In Thee is my help, Lord, and only in Thee.

Fain would I be cheerful, and sing as I go,
   Uplifting Thy praises through darkness and
      dawn ;
Fain wear a white robe, not the garment of
      woe,
   And joyously, blithely, and gayly go on.
Oh, bid me to triumph and smile through my
      tears,
Oh, crown me a victor o'er trials and fears.
My Master, my Master, my joy is in Thee,
In Thee is my help, Lord, and only in Thee.

GOING HOME

OUT of the chill and the shadow
  Into the thrill and the shine ;
Out of the dearth and the famine
  Into the fulness divine.
Up from the strife and the battle
  (Oft with the shameful defeat),
Up to the palm and the laurel,
  Oh, but the rest will be sweet !

Leaving the cloud and the tempest,
  Reaching the balm and the cheer,
Finding the end of our sorrow,
  Finding the end of our fear.
Seeing the face of the Master
  Yearned for in " distance and dream,"
Oh, for that rapture of gladness !
  Oh, for that vision supreme !

Meeting the dear ones departed,
  Knowing them, clasping their hands,

All the beloved and true-hearted,
  There in the fairest of lands!
Sin evermore left behind us,
  Pain nevermore to distress;
Changing the moan for the music,
  Living the Saviour to bless.

Why should we fear at the dying
  That is but springing to life,
Why should we shrink from the struggle,
  Pale at the swift closing strife,
Since it is only beyond us,
  Scarcely a step, and a breath,
All that dear home of the living,
  Guarded by what we call death!

There we shall learn the sweet meanings
  Hidden to-day from our eyes.
There we shall waken like children
  Joyous at gift and surprise.
Come, then, dear Lord, in the gloaming,
  Or when the dawning is gray!
Take us to dwell in Thy presence—
  Only Thyself lead the way.

Out of the chill and the shadow
  Into the thrill and the shine;
Out of the dearth and the famine
  Into the fulness divine.

Out of the sigh and the silence
  Into the deep-swelling song ;
Out of the exile and bondage
  Into the home-gathered throng.

III
THANKSGIVING

IN THE OLD HOME

Like the patient moss to the rifted hill,
 The wee brown house is clinging,
A last year's nest that is lone and still,
 Though it erst was filled with singing.
Then fleet were the children's pattering feet,
 And their trilling childish laughter,
And merry voices, were sweet, oh, sweet,
 Ringing from floor to rafter.

The beautiful darlings one by one,
 From the nest's safe shelter flying,
Went forth in sheen of the morning sun,
 Their fluttering pinions trying.
But oft as the reaping-time is o'er,
 And the hoar frost crisps the stubble,
They haste to the little home once more
 From the great world's toil and trouble.

And the mother herself is at the pane,
 With a hand the dim eyes shading,
And the flush of girlhood tints again
 The cheek that is thin and fading.

For the boys and girls are coming home,
  Their mother's kiss their guerdon,
As they came ere yet they had learned to
    roam
  Or bowed to the task and burden.

Over the door's worn sill they troop,
  The skies of youth above them,
The blessing of God on the happy group,
  Who have mother left to love them.
They well may smile in the face of care,
  To whom such grace is given;
A mother's faith and a mother's prayer
  Holding them close to Heaven.

For her, as she clasps her bearded son,
  With a heart that's brimming over,
She's tenderly blending two in one,
  Her boy and her boyish lover.
And half of her soul is reft away—
  So twine the dead and the living,
In the little home wherein to-day
  Her children keep Thanksgiving.

There are tiny hands that pull her gown,
  And small heads bright and golden;
The childish laugh and the childish frown,
  And the dimpled fingers folden,

That bring again to the mother breast.
    The spell of the sunny weather,
When she hushed her brood in the crowded
        nest
    And all were glad together.

A truce to the jarring notes of life,
    The cries of pain and passion.
Over this lull in the eager strife,
    Love hovers, Eden fashion.
In the wee brown house were lessons taught
    Of strong and sturdy living,
And ever where honest hands have wrought,
    God hears the true Thanksgiving.

THANKSGIVING ALWAYS

WHEN barn and byre are safe,
  When flocks are in the fold,
When far and near the burdened fields
  Have bowed 'neath harvest's gold,
When clusters rich have drooped
  From many a blushing vine,
And genial orchards, wide and fair,
  Have owned the touch divine,
Then, up from grateful hearts
  Let joyful praise arise
To Him who gives the waiting earth
  The blessing of the skies.

When round the mother's knee
  The little children cling,
When night and morn the household eaves
  With merry voices ring,
When not a sunny head
  Is missing from the throng,
When not a silver note is dropped
  From out the daily song,

Then, up from thankful hearts
   Let fervent praise arise
To Him who fills the happy home
   With blessing from the skies.

When round the white-haired man,
   Serene in stately age,
The children's children troop to crown
   His lengthened pilgrimage,
When through translucent air
   The gentle matron sees
How love and peace have followed her
   While striving God to please,
Then, up from reverent hearts
   Let psalms of praise arise
To Him who keeps His promises
   In blessing from the skies.

When blight is on the field,
   When storms are o'er the hills,
When leap, in wildest fury tossed,
   The late rejoicing rills,
When wealth is on the wane,
   And battle finds defeat,
When bitterness o'erbrims the cup
   That erst was foaming sweet,
Ah! then? Yea, then, let thanks
   From all believers rise

III

To Him whose chariot is the clouds,
  Who reigns above the skies.

When rosebud lips are pale,
  And household mirth is hushed,
When o'er a tiny coffin lid .
  The bliss of life is crushed,
When breaks the staff of strength
  And snaps the beauteous rod,
Or worse—when dear ones go astray
  And leave their father's God,
"Even so, Thy will be done,"
  The Christian's heart shall say,
And find that will a central sun
  To light the darkest day.

Come pleasure's tide at flood,
  Come loss and grief and pain,
Come death and parting—God is good,
  So lift we up the strain
Of thanks to Him who keeps
  His own in storm and calm,
And who with dearth, or wound, or cross,
  Aye sends a healing balm.
All days should therefore be
  Thanksgivings to the Wise,
The True, the Kind, the Sovereign hand,
  That rules us from the skies.

MOTHER'S THANKSGIVING

Such a quaint little Mother, in a gown of
    silver gray,
Her snowy hair smooth-parted, in the dear
    old-fashioned way,
And on her head a lint-white cap, of softest,
    filmiest lace,
That made a picture-frame about her sweet
    and placid face.

Such a brave little Mother! So many a
    year had fled
Since her husband, leal and loving, had been
    numbered with the dead.
So many, many summers had she borne a
    lonely heart
That her fair age and his bright youth were
    half a life apart.

Such a gentle little Mother! Ah! the boys
    remember now,
Sorrowfully, every shadow on that tender,
    tranquil brow.

They remember how she taught them, how
    she kissed them each at night,
And they felt no need of angels keeping
    watch till morning light.

Such a trustful little Mother! There were
    dark days now and then,
Though the dear lads never dreamed it until
    they were bearded men;
She would go away alone, kneeling in her
    chamber dim,
And would tell the Lord her troubles, cast-
    ing all her care on Him.

Such a happy little Mother! With a laugh
    like bells a-chime,
Ever swift to see the bright side, ready with
    a quip and rhyme.
Oh, so quick with love's own pity! oh, so
    earnest 'neath the jest!
Ever lavishing her kindness, giving ever of
    her best.

Such a winsome little Mother! Why, the
    village children came
Trooping merrily about her; she knew every
    one by name;

Baby faces smiled to greet hers, by some
    subtle impulse stirred,
As if fledglings knew the brooding of the
    tender mother-bird.

Such a true little Mother! Never dallying
    with wrong ;
Honest to the very soul's core ; bearing bur-
    dens late and long ;
Paying every debt with interest ; filling every
    day with work,
With a deep disdain for any who the day's
    demand would shirk.

Such a blessed little Mother! Through their
    tears her sons to-day
Thank the God she served and honored that
    she sleeping passed away ;
Lifted to the home in heaven, to the com-
    rade gone before,
Just as earth's Thanksgiving greetings floated
    through the open door

COMMON MERCIES

Dear Lord, are we ever so thankful,
   As thankful as we should be to Thee,
For Thine angels sent down to defend us
   From dangers our eyes never see ;
From perils that lurk unsuspected,
   The powers of earth and of air,
The while we are heaven-protected
   And guarded from evil and snare ?

Are we grateful, as grateful we should be,
   For commonplace days of delight,
When safe we fare forth to our labor,
   And safe we fare homeward at night ;
For the weeks in which nothing has hap-
     pened
   Save commonplace toiling and play,
When we've worked at the tasks of the
     household,
   And peace hushed the house day by day?

Dear Lord, that the terror at midnight,
    The weird of the wind and the flame,
Hath passed by our dwelling, we praise Thee,
    And lift up our hearts in Thy name ;
That the circle of darlings unbroken
    Yet gathers in bliss round the board,
That commonplace love is our portion,
    We give Thee our praises, dear Lord !

Forgive us who live by Thy bounty,
    That often our lives are so bare
Of the garlands of praise that should render
    All votive and fragrant each prayer.
Dear Lord, in the sharpness of trouble
    We cry from the depths to the throne !
In the long days of gladness and beauty,
    Take Thou the glad hearts as Thine own.

Oh, common are sunshine and flowers,
    And common are raindrop and dew,
And the gay little footsteps of children,
    And common the love that holds true.
So, Lord, for our commonplace mercies,
    That straight from Thy hand are bestowed,
We are fain to uplift our thanksgivings—
    Take, Lord, the long debt we have owed.

IV

CHRISTMAS SONGS

HER GIFTS

A DEAR little mother is waiting apart—
    The mother of children three.
"My Lord," she cries, in the hush of her heart,
    "Wilt Thou take a gift from me?
I have heard the angels sing Thy birth,
    I have followed Thy shining star,
And here at the shrine of all the earth,
    Lo! I and my children are.

" And all in the glow of the Christmas morn,
    My gold to lay at Thy feet,
I am leading my darlings with care unworn,
    With brows that are pure and sweet.
Oh, never had gems from the mines such worth
    As the treasure to-day I bring
To the beautiful shrine of all the earth,
    To the glorious Infant King.

"My children three, with their waving hair
    And the fearless look in their eyes,
They lisp thy name in the vesper prayer,
    And at matins when they rise.

121

Nothing they know of the dole and dearth
  Of souls that with sin have striven ;
They kneel at the shrine of all the earth—
  ' Of such is the kingdom of heaven.' "

They stand in the shadow of pine and fir ;
  They listen, and, floating through,
They catch the answer that's sent to her
  Through a rift in the upper blue :
" Since the Christ-child came to the weary
      earth
  No gifts are to Him so sweet
As the children's hearts, with their joy and
      mirth,
  Lovingly brought to His feet.

THE ANNUNCIATION

WITH grave eyes rapt in dreams of prayer,
   She sits alone within the room,
Unheeding if around her there
   Be golden ray or deepening gloom.
Her heart uplifted, silent, sweet,
Her thought goes forth her Lord to greet.

And thus attent before the King,
   No sense of strangeness startles her
When one from Heaven draws near to bring
   A sign to Heaven's worshipper.
"Hail, Mary!" fills her soul with bliss,
Her tranquil years have waited this.

Behold a lily in his hand,
   A lily by the angels sown,
With fragrance from the deathless land;
   This lily, in God's garden grown,
Salutes her purity, as white
As robes the saints wear in God's sight.

Oh, sacred grace of motherhood!
  Divinest thing beneath the sky,
Which yet the heavens overbrood,
  The watching angels hovering nigh.
Unending rite of sacrifice,
Costly beyond earth's utmost price.

"Hail, Mary!" thrills each mother soul;
  Ere yet the life beat faint and sweet,
That shall not cease while ages roll,
  Each mother hears the glad repeat,
And thenceforth, hallowed, dwells apart,
Heaven's matchless lily in her heart.

THE STAR OF BETHLEHEM

WHAT became of the Star, the Bethlehem
　　Star,
　That was followed by kings and sages
As they journeyed o'er desert and mountain
　　far,
　To find the Pearl of the Ages?

Did the angels quench its torch of fire
　In the first sweet Christmas dawn,
When they sang to the world of the world's
　　desire,
　Ere the night from the hills had gone?

Did it suddenly vanish into space,
　Blown out, when its golden ray
Had bathed in glory the lonely place
　Where the Child and mother lay?

And since I wonder, but cannot tell,
　Some day to come I shall know;

It may guide the steps of the wise who dwell
  Where the heavenly mansions glow,

When they shut their eyes on the lamps of
    earth,
  And with silent feet unshod,
Go forth to look for the Father's hearth
  In the beautiful City of God.

It well may be the Bethlehem Star
  Shines out across their way,
Leading them safe, or near, or far,
  To the Prince of the deathless day.

Oh! Star that over the manger stood
  The night when Christ was born,
When the Only Potent, the Only Good,
  Came down to this world forlorn.

Still shine in the heart of mother and child
  Wherever love reigns and sings,
And the face of a little one undefiled
  Hath that which may conquer kings.

Oh! Bethlehem Star, through pain and loss,
  Still over the cradle shine,
And comfort us if a shadowy cross
  There glimmer in faint outline.

For we cannot but take the self-same path
  That was trodden by kings and sages,
When they dared the base world's utmost
      wrath,
  And sought the Pearl of the Ages.

WHEN CHRISTMAS COMES

When Christmas comes,
The baby girl who scarce can speak,
The youth with bronzed and bearded cheek,
The aged bent with weight of years,
The sorrow-stricken spent with tears,
The poor, the rich, the grave, the gay,
Who fare along life's rugged way,
Are glad of heart when, in the sky,
The wondrous seraph wings sweep by,
 When Christmas comes.

When Christmas comes,
The sailor on the seas afloat,
The traveller in lands remote,
The warrior by the camp-fire's light,
The courtier in the palace bright,
The student by the midnight lamp,
The miner deep in dust and damp,
Alike uplift, through riven skies,
The wondering look of glad surprise,
 When Christmas comes.

When Christmas comes,
In field and street, in mart and farm,
The world takes on a lovelier charm ;
Sweet-scented boughs of pine and fir
Are brought, like frankincense and myrrh,
To make our hallowed places meet
For hands that clasp and tones that greet,
While hearts, worth more than gold or gem,
Go forth to find their Bethlehem,
When Christmas comes.

CHRISTMAS EVE

WELL, John, we will hang up our stockings—
  There are only you and I
To keep alive the Yule-log,
  As the lonely years go by.
Once we had quite a dozen
  To hang in a cheerful row,
Where the good Saint Nicholas packed his
    gifts
  Snugly from knee to toe.

There were four for our fathers and mothers,
  Both of us had them then,
And we drove in a nail for Cousin Ruth,
  And another for Uncle Ben.
And the dear little children followed,
  And then came yours and mine;
I can see that row of stockings,
  Through my gathering tears they shine.

Oh! sweet in the dusk of twilight,
  Were our Christmas Eves, dear John!

And merry and gay were our Christmas morns
  In the years that I think upon.
For old and young together
  Were merry and blithe and gay,
In the whirl of the blessed old-time
  When we kept our Christmas day.

We two have grown grave and silent,
  Though we have not grown apart.
You are more to me than the whole wide
     world,
  I more to you, sweetheart!
But the children are men and women,
  With their own full lives to live;
And they've only a moment now and then,
  To the old home nest to give.

And a furrowed ridge, in the grave-yard,
  Covers the bit of earth
Where they sleep, through snow and sun-
    shine,
  The dear ones who gave us birth.
The world is narrowing in, John,
  It will be our turn to go
Some Christmas Eve, in the gloaming,
  When the lights are dim and low.

But we'll not be sorrowful, darling—
  You mind the dear old tune,

That we sang with tripping tongues, love,
  When our sun was at its noon.
For I think we'll hear the angels,
  As the gates of pearl swing wide,
And we step ashore in the morning
  On the river's farther side.

So, John, we will yet keep Christmas,
  And bid the Yule-log glow,
And crowd our stockings with presents,
  Lovingly, heel and toe.
Perhaps the dear Saint, passing,
  Will smile a little to see
How much like merry children
  A happy old pair can be.

GOD BLESS US ALL

God bless us all! With Tiny Tim
'Tis thus we finish prayer and hymn,
While cheerily from lip to lip
The Christmas wishes gayly trip ;
God bless us all, the circle round,
Wherever are our dear ones found ;
At home, abroad, please God, we say,
God bless His own on Christmas Day!

God bless the golden heads arow
Where ruddy hearth flames leap and glow ;
God bless the baby hands that clasp
Heart fibres in their clinging grasp ;
God bless the youth with eager gaze ;
God bless the sage of lengthened days ;
At home, abroad, please God, we cry,
God guard His own, 'neath any sky!

God ease the weary ones who bear
A cumbering weight of grief and care ;

137

God give the wage no ill can spoil,
The honest loaf for honest toil ;
We sound the heartfelt prayer and hymn,
And breathe " Amen," with Tiny Tim,
As reverently, please God, we say,
God bless us all on Christmas Day !

V
EASTER

AN EASTER SONG

Sing a song of Easter,
  A song of happy hours,
Of dashing spray, and shadow play,
  And lovely springing flowers,
Of birds come home again to build
  Beside the cottage eaves,
Of waking buds, and rushing floods,
  And dance of rustling leaves.

Sing a song of Easter,
  A song that means a prayer
Of want and love to One above
  Who keeps His world in care ;
A song for all on this green earth,
  For dear ones passed away,
Sing clear and strong the joyful song,
  The song of Easter Day.

Sing a song of Easter,
  A song of pure delight,

A song that starts in merry hearts,
  And swells from morn till night ;
An Easter song that children lift,
  Without a jarring chord,   -
That thrills afar from star to star,
  To praise the children's Lord.

MARY

SHE walked amid the lilies
  Upstanding straight and tall,
Their silver tapers bright against
  The dusky mountain wall;
Gray olives dropped upon her
  Their crystal globes of dew,
The while the doors of heaven grew wide
  To let the Easter through.

All heaven was rose and golden,
  The clouds were reft apart,
Earth's holiest dawn in dazzling white
  Came forth from heaven's own heart;
And never, since on Eden
  Creation's glory lay,
Had ever garden of the Lord
  Beheld so fair a day.

Her eyes were blurred with weeping,
  Her trailing steps were slow;

The cross she bore within her
  Transfixed her soul with woe.
One only goal before her
  Loomed through her spirit's gloom,
As in the early morning
  She sought the guarded tomb.

But down the lilied pathway
  A kingly presence came,
A seamless garment clothed Him,
  His face was clear as flame,
And in His hands were nail-prints,
  And on His brow were scars,
But in His eyes a light of love
  Beyond the light of stars.

For tears she could not see Him,
  As o'er the path He came,
Till, like remembered music,
  He called her by her name ;
Then swift her soul to answer,
  The Lord of life she knew,
Her breast unbarred its prison gates
  To let the Easter through.

Such light of revelation
  As bathed her being then,
It comes anew wherever Christ
  Is known indeed of men ;

Such glory on the pathway,
  It falls again on all
Who hear the King in blessing,
  And hasten at His call.

Rise, King of grace and glory,
  This hallowed Easter-tide,
Nor from Thy ransomed people
  Let even death divide ;
For yet again doth heaven
  Throw all its gates apart,
And send the sacred Easter
  Straight from its glowing heart.

K

THE END